MYSTERY OF THE MASKS

ADAPTED BY KATE HOWARD

ISBN 978-1-338-22791-8

10 9 8 7 6 5 4 3 2 1   18 19 20 21 22

Printed in the U.S.A.   40

First printing 2018

SCHOLASTIC INC.

CELEBRATING DRAGON DAY

Crowds filled the streets of Ninjago City.
Everyone was busy celebrating Dragon Day.
No one noticed a group of masked figures sneaking through the crowd.

As fireworks exploded in the sky, the masked figures climbed to the top of Borg Tower.

They were on a mission to steal something very valuable.

Inside, the masked intruders quickly found what they were looking for.

It was an all-powerful Oni Mask!

One thief grabbed the mask from its case, and an alarm went off.

Laser beams lit up the room. Steel walls slammed down.

With the mask in their hands, the thieves took off running.

ENTER THE NINJA

The group of masked figures raced across the roof of Borg Tower.

But another masked figure stopped them.

It was Lloyd, the Green Ninja!

The Green Ninja took down the bad guys one by one. But before he could grab the Oni Mask, one of the thieves escaped! The mysterious figure slipped through the crowd and took off on a motorcycle.

Lloyd hopped onto his motorbike. The chase was on!

Lloyd followed the thief through Ninjago City.

"Who am I chasing?" he asked Pixal, the ninja's AI system.

"He or she is not in our database," Pixal replied.

"I need backup," Lloyd said.

"The ninja are on other missions," Pixal told him. "You are on your own."

The thief sped through traffic. Lloyd was hot on his tail.

Suddenly, the bad guy's motorcycle zoomed off the edge of a bridge!

The thief opened a parachute and floated down into a waiting speedboat.

It was too late to catch him.

"Master Lloyd?" Pixal said. "Are you all right? Are you there?"

"Yeah, I'm here," Lloyd said. "It's time to get the team back together."

He had something important to tell his friends.

Lloyd needed the whole team to track down the thief and get the mask back.

"Master Lloyd requires your attention in Ninjago City," Pixal told the other ninja.

"Is it serious?" asked Zane, the Master of Ice.

"It appears so," Pixal said.

Kai and Zane were busy fighting an old enemy. But Zane knew Lloyd only asked for help when he really needed it.

"We will be there shortly," Zane told Pixal.

Then he hit the enemy with an icy blast so he and Kai could return to Ninjago City.

TOGETHER AGAIN

Lloyd, Cole, Jay, Kai, Nya, and Zane gathered at Borg Tower.

"Thanks for meeting me," Lloyd said. "I called you all here because of this."

Lloyd showed them the symbol he'd seen on the thief's parachute. It was a picture of Garmadon, his father.

"That is the symbol for the Sons of Garmadon!" Zane said. "They are a mysterious criminal group in Ninjago City."

"Three days ago, this group stole a powerful mask from Borg Tower," said Lloyd.

Just then, a man named Mr. Hutchins walked into the room.

"The mask that was stolen is an Oni Mask. There are only three in all," he told the ninja.

"I'm confused," said Jay. "How can there be *three* masks when you just said it's the *only* mask?"

"Not 'only,' Jay," Nya said. "*Oni.*"

"The Oni are all-powerful beings," Zane explained. "They are demons that have been around longer than Ninjago Island."

Mr. Hutchins nodded. "Each mask embodies one of three Oni warlords. If all three masks are united, their owner will have great power."

"Mr. Hutchins serves the royal family," Lloyd told his team.

Mr. Hutchins nodded. "The Emperor is giving a public speech tomorrow. I am worried the Sons of Garmadon may try to steal his Oni Mask. We need your help protecting it."

THE ROYAL FAMILY

The next day, the ninja arrived at the Royal Palace just in time for the Emperor's speech.

"As many of you know," the Emperor told the crowd, "my family has kept a private life. But with the rise in crime, it is time for us to step out of the shadows and into the light."

During the Emperor's speech, the ninja scanned the crowd. They were looking for signs of trouble.

"Master Lloyd has spotted something of interest," Zane said.

Sure enough, Lloyd's eyes were fixed on the stage.

Kai chuckled. "Looks like Lloyd's got an eye for the princess."

"Let's just do our job," Lloyd said, ignoring Kai. "The Emperor is almost finished. Be on the lookout."

Suddenly, a balloon floated up out of the crowd. It turned in the wind, revealing the Sons of Garmadon symbol!

Pop! Pop! Pop!

Three loud blasts rang out nearby. The crowd screamed and ran.

Lloyd raced to the stage to protect the royal family.

Once they were safe, Lloyd asked his team, "Is the threat clear?"

"It was just firecrackers. False alarm," Nya called.

"You protected the royal family," Mr. Hutchins told the ninja. "They wish to thank you. You are invited to be their guests in the palace."

INSIDE THE PALACE

"Welcome to the Royal Palace," Mr. Hutchins said, leading the ninja inside. "It is also known as the Palace of Secrets."

"Why do they call it the Palace of Secrets?" Kai asked.

Mr. Hutchins frowned. "If I told you that, then it wouldn't be a secret."

Mr. Hutchins guided the ninja to the throne room. "I present to you, the Emperor and Empress of Ninjago, and their daughter, the Jade Princess— Princess Harumi."

Princess Harumi greeted the ninja. "I have read much about each of you. Your heroics will surely become legend."

The Jade Princess stepped over to meet Nya. "Nya, you are the girl I've always wanted to be. I admire your mastery of water and your skills that rival any man."

"I like her," Nya said, grinning.

"Our daughter would like you to stay with us until the threat is over," the Empress told the ninja.

"As long as we have an Oni Mask, we fear our lives are in danger," said the Emperor.

"The masks must never be reunited," Princess Harumi said.

"We are happy to help," Lloyd said.

THE PALACE OF SECRETS

Mr. Hutchins led the ninja on a tour of the palace. "The palace is equipped with secret passages," he told them.

"Ah!" Kai said. "So that's why it's called the Palace of Secrets."

"Yes," Mr. Hutchins said, frowning. "But only the royal family knows the location of these secret passages."

As the tour continued, Nya whispered, "Anyone else think there's something a little off about this Hutchins guy?"

Lloyd nodded. He had been thinking the same thing! "He's holding something back . . ."

Mr. Hutchins led the group into an exhibit hall. "Finally, the reason we need your protection: the Mask of Deception."

"Ugh," Kai said, gazing at the mask. "That's a face only a mother could love. Why would anyone want that?"

"That's what we need to figure out," Lloyd said.

"If this is the Mask of Deception, what was stolen from Borg Tower?" Nya asked.

"The Mask of Vengeance," Mr. Hutchins said.

"Who has the third Oni Mask?" Cole asked.

"No one knows the location of the Mask of Hatred," Zane explained. "But my sensors tell me it will not be lost for long . . ."

"Zane is correct," Mr. Hutchins said. "No one has found the third mask, but we know dark forces are looking for it. That's why we need eyes on *this mask* at all times."

Later that night, Lloyd walked past Princess Harumi's quarters. Her door was wide open.

"Princess Harumi, are you there?" he called out.

No one answered, so Lloyd stepped inside.

The window was wide open. The room was a mess. And the princess . . . was gone!